Settling Down

Book 8: Colorado Heritage Series

Sybil Downing
and
Jane Valentine Barker

PRUETT PUBLISHING COMPANY
Boulder, Colorado 80301

©1979 by Jane Valentine Barker and Sybil Downing
All rights reserved, including those to reproduce this book, or parts thereof, in any form without permission in writing from the Publisher.

Library of Congress Catalog Card No. 79-90265

Illustrations by Robert F. Wilson

First Edition
1 2 3 4 5 6 7 8 9

ISBN: 0-87108-227-6

Printed in the United States of America

Acknowledgments

We want to thank the following people for sharing their professional expertise, and for their kindness and encouragement in this project:

Dr. Maxine Benson, Curator of Documentary Resources, Colorado Historical Society

Ms. Catherine Engel, librarian, Documentary Resources, Colorado Historical Society

Jane Fitz-Randolph, author and teacher

Nancy Markham, Curator of Education, Colorado State Historical Society

Roger Martinez, Director, Multi-Ethnic Studies, Colorado Department of Education

Denver 1860s—*Courtesy Colorado Historical Society*

Treasure From The Ashes

Denver, Colorado
April 1863

Louis finished sweeping the floor of the tiny barbershop. His father, Barney Ford, was giving the last customer of the day a shave.

"Barney," said the thin, younger man, "I want to thank you for keeping your shop open tonight. I'm meeting some men for dinner, and I wanted to look my best."

"No trouble, Mr. Kountz," said Louis' father. "You're a good customer. Anyway, I have Louis to help me clean up. So it's no extra trouble."

"You know, Barney," said Mr. Kountz, "you're a hard worker. Your whole family is hard working. You'll do well out here in Denver, now that it's growing so fast."

"Well, I thank you for the kind words," said Louis' father. "I really don't want to be a barber all my life. You know I once owned a restaurant. But there's not much choice for a colored man like me, even out here in the territories. I tried mining up in Mountain City, and the white men jumped my claim. If only I could start another restaurant."

"I don't blame you for feeling low, Barney," said Luther Kountz. "But things are getting a little better. Why, you and the other colored men in Colorado Territory just voted for the first time last year. Besides, everyone in town thinks most highly of you."

"I thank you again for your kind words, Mr. Kountz," said Barney. "But the future must hold more than kind words for me and my family." He finished patting his customer's face dry.

"Well, I wish you the best, my friend," said Mr. Kountz. "And now, it's good night. And good night to you, Louis."

"Good night, sir," answered Louis, as he pulled down the shade over the front window. He was glad Mr. Kountz and his father had stopped talking. The smell of his mother's good stew came from the kitchen in the back, and he was hungry.

The Ford family lived in quarters behind the barbershop on F Street. They used to live in Chicago, but Louis' father thought there was more chance for them here in the West.

As soon as Louis' mother finished washing the dishes, she put baby Sara to bed, and Louis and his father played chess.

Barney Ford—*Courtesy Colorado Historical Society*

"Daddy, you always win," said Louis. "Let's play one more game. I'll bet I can beat you this time."

"No, Louis," answered his father. "Not tonight. We all need our rest." He picked up the kerosene lamp and turned to go into the little bedroom. Louis slept on a cot in the kitchen. Now he undressed in the dark room and crept into the bed.

The next thing he knew, his father was shaking him. "Wake up, Louis!" he said, anxiously. "A fire! A bad one! I am sending your mother and the baby over to our friends, the Sanderlins. But we have to help fight the blaze." He gasped for breath. "Our store may be next to go."

Louis pulled on his pants and boots and struggled into his coat. Shouts came from the street. Louis and his father ran out the door of the barbershop. People ran in every direction. The air was filled with smoke. Flames shot up from the buildings across the street.

A long line of men stretched down the street. They were passing buckets of water from Cherry Creek to throw on the burning buildings.

"We need more water to put out the fire, Daddy!" shouted Louis.

"The bucket brigade is trying its best, son," said his father. "But there isn't enough water to

do much good. See, people are throwing sand on the fire. It's better than nothing. We'd better go help the other men cart more sand from the edge of the creek."

All night, Louis and Mr. Ford worked frantically with the other men. The burning timbers crackled. Walls of buildings suddenly would buckle and fall into the street. The heat was almost too much for Louis as he threw sand onto the flames.

By early morning nothing but piles of ashes and smoldering timbers lay where wooden buildings had been before. Only the few brick buildings were left standing.

"Oh, Daddy," said Louis, staring around

him. "What will we do? There is nothing left."

Louis' father slowly took a large handkerchief from his pocket. He began to wipe black soot from his face. "Well, son," he said, "we will just have to figure out something, won't we? But right now, I think we should go over to the Sanderlins and try to rest."

Louis and his father trudged several blocks until they reached some houses. "I guess we're all lucky the wind didn't shift last night," said Louis' father. "These houses might have burned too."

The two walked up to a small white house. Even before they reached the porch, the door opened. Louis' mother raced out and hugged Louis and her husband.

"Oh, Barney! Louis!" she cried. "Thank heaven, you're both all right! Did the barbershop burn down?"

Louis' father nodded, sadly.

"You both look so tired. I have some water heating," said Louis' mother. "Once you're clean and can get some sleep, things will seem better."

The Sanderlin family was still sleeping. Quietly, Louis' father lay down on the sofa in the living room. Louis tried to sleep on the bedroll his mother had put down on the back porch. But he just stared up at the ceiling for a long time. He kept thinking about their barbershop. After awhile he felt his eyelids growing heavy. He fell into a deep sleep.

When Louis woke up, he wondered for a moment where he was. Then he remembered. He sat up and pulled on his boots. He reached for his coat and slipped out the back door.

As Louis hurried down the street, the air stung his eyes and throat. Ahead he could still see wisps of black smoke.

At Blake and F streets, Louis stopped and looked around. Here and there men were poking through the ashes. Louis had a sinking feeling in the pit of his stomach. If only something was left at their barbershop.

Suddenly he heard a deep voice. "Louis, what are you doing here?" asked his father.

"I just thought maybe I could find something, Daddy," answered Louis.

"Oh, there's nothing left, son," said his father. "You just go on back to the Sanderlins. I'm going over to talk to Luther Kountz. I'm going to ask to borrow some money to rebuild the barbershop."

"But his bank was just down the street from our shop, Daddy," said Louis. "It burned down, too."

"It sure did," said his father. "But do you know that Mr. Kountz has already opened his bank again. In the back of the brick building over there. Can you beat that?"

"But if his bank burned, where would he get the money to run his bank?" asked Louis.

"Well, I don't really know, son," answered his father. "Maybe he saved the bags of gold dust from the fire."

"I guess lots of other people will need money, won't they?" asked Louis. "Do you think Mr. Kountz has that much money in his bank?"

"Hard to say, Louis," answered his father. "Anyway, you get back to your mother." He walked across the street toward the brick building. Louis watched his father make his way through the crowd of men standing by the door. He thought his father walked just as a king would walk.

Turning, Louis started up the street. Then he stopped and looked back at the pile of burned timbers where the barbershop had stood. He just had to look. He walked back and began to pick his way over the debris.

Suddenly his shoe hit something hard. Louis leaned down and felt around. His fingers touched something. A metal box. Louis held his breath. He pulled it out. Dusting off the ashes, he carefully pried open the lid. Inside were razors and scissors. His father's barber tools. Closing the box, he put it under his arm and ran up the street toward the Sanderlins.

Louis was just about to knock when Mrs. Sanderlin opened the front door. "Well, I'm glad to see you, Louis," she said. "Your mother and I fixed a good dinner and no one is here to eat it."

"I saw Daddy awhile ago," said Louis. "He said he was going to see Mr. Kountz, the banker. But there were so many other men waiting too. Maybe Daddy is still waiting to get into see him."

"I don't see how he has any chance to borrow money," said Louis' mother, shaking her head. "We still owe money on the land where the barbershop was standing."

Just then footsteps sounded on the porch. Mr. Ford burst into the room. "You will never guess my good news!" he exclaimed, beaming.

"You got the money, Daddy?" asked Louis. "For the barbershop?"

"Indeed I did get the money, Louis," answered his father. "But not for the barbershop."

Louis caught his breath. "Not for the barbershop?" he said, anxiously.

"No sir, not for the barbershop," his father said again. "But I'm so hungry, I don't think I'm strong enough to tell what happened right now. Why don't we eat some of that good dinner I smell in the kitchen first."

Everyone sat down at the table and began to eat. "Daddy, couldn't you tell just a little of the story now?" begged Louis.

"No, not yet," said his father. He seemed to chew each mouthful of his meat and potatoes and stewed tomatoes a hundred times. Finally he pushed aside his empty plate.

"Now, Daddy?" asked Louis.

"All right, Louis," agreed his father. "I guess I'm able to tell the story after that good meal. Well, as you know, there was a large crowd in front of the store. I could hardly make my way to the door. But the minute Mr. Kountz saw me, he waved for me to come ahead of everyone else waiting to see him. I can tell you, some of the men were pretty mad about that." He smiled and shook his head.

"Anyway," he went on. "I came right out and asked Mr. Kountz for the money to rebuild the barbershop. For a few minutes he just sat there and stared at me. And then he said, 'No. No money for the barbershop.' Well, I didn't know what to do. So I just said, 'Thank you, anyway,' and started to leave."

Louis wished his father would hurry and get to the point.

"Then all of a sudden Mr. Kountz said, 'Just a minute, Barney Ford. I said no money for the barbershop. But for the restaurant you want to start, you can have ten thousand dollars. Just on your signature.' "

" 'On your signature'?" asked Louis. "What does that mean, Daddy?"

"It means, son," answered his father, "that Mr. Kountz trusts me. He trusts me so much that all I have to do is sign my name on a paper. The paper says I will return the money by a certain time. Usually people must give the banker the deed to their house until they pay the money back."

Louis wasn't sure he really understood about borrowing money. But he knew Mr. Kountz must really like his father. "Tell the rest of the story, Daddy," he urged.

"Where was I?" asked his father. "Oh, yes. Well, I could hardly believe my ears. Ten thousand dollars, just on my signature! So I asked Mr. Kountz why he would do such a thing, and Mr. Kountz said to me, 'Barney, I told you I think you will go far here in Denver. You're a hard worker. You're honest. You're well liked. I know you ran a restaurant once before so you know the business.' "

"And then what?" asked Louis.

"Hold on, son," said his father. "I'm getting there. So then Mr. Kountz said 'With this fire, Denver will need a new restaurant. You will do a fine job. It's just good business for me to let you have that money, Barney.' "

As his father finished the story, Louis remembered the box of barber tools.

"Daddy, I found something from the fire," he said. "But I guess they won't help much now." He lifted the box down from the shelf.

His father opened the box. He picked up the scissors and razors and then put each one back.

"Louis," he said, "I can't tell you how much this box means to me. I used these tools for many years. Even though I won't be using them now, it is fine to have them." He got up and hugged Louis.

"You have always been a fine help to me, son," said his father. "Now you can help me in our new business—the restaurant business. In fact, I think it might be a good idea for you to give our new business a name."

Smiling, Louis remembered what Mr. Kountz had said about Denver growing. New people came into town every day now. Lots of people. That was it. "Daddy," said Louis, "let's call our restaurant the 'People Restaurant.'"

Antlers Hotel—*Courtesy Denver Public Library, Western History Department*

Dry as a Bone

Colorado Springs, Colorado
June 1885

"Nothing exciting ever happens around here, Tim," moaned Jeannie Smith. She sat on the front steps of the hotel and patted the little brown dog lying beside her.

"Boy, that's the truth," agreed her big brother. He stretched his long legs in front of him and leaned back on his elbows. Squinting a little in the bright afternoon sun, he watched the wagons and carriages going along Pike's Peak Avenue. The horses hooves kicked up little clouds of dust in the dirt street.

"Wouldn't a picnic be fun?" suggested Jeannie. "You know, a really big picnic. With all the families here at the hotel."

"I guess so," admitted Tim, "but where would we go?"

"How about that place Daddy told us about—with all the funny-shaped rocks?" answered Jeannie.

"Oh, you mean the Garden of the Gods," said Tim. "Yeah, that would be okay. But that's kind of far away. Six or seven miles, I've heard."

"Maybe we could rent carriages," said Jeannie hopefully.

"Maybe," said Tim, "and I'll just bet you want that dumb dog of yours to come."

"Of course Toby would come," said Jeannie. "And, anyway, he's not dumb. I'm going to find Daddy and tell him my idea." She scooped up the little terrier and walked across the big porch.

As she let the heavy front door close behind her, Jeannie stood for a minute trying to see in the dim light of the big lobby. Her whole family had come out from Philadelphia to spend the summer here at the new Antlers Hotel. Mother said it would be good for them to get out of the heat of the big city and breathe the good fresh air of Colorado Springs. The town was still small, but people liked to come for vacations.

Jeannie liked the hotel well enough. It had all kinds of special rooms—a music room, dining rooms, a billiard room, even two bathrooms on each floor. And there were other girls and boys to play with too. But she thought the weather was just as hot as in Philadelphia. And, so far, there certainly wasn't very much to do.

No one seemed to be around. But she could hear a man's deep voice off in the parlor. Then the sound of people clapping. She remembered a minister was to give some kind of talk to the grownups this afternoon.

In a few minutes her mother and father came through the parlor doorway. "Mother! Daddy!" Jeannie called. "I have the best idea!"

"Oh, you do, do you," laughed her father. His thick dark beard tickled as he kissed her on the forehead.

"A picnic. For everybody," said Jeannie. "Out by all those funny rocks."

Mother looked at Daddy, smiling. "You know, Alfred, I think Jeannie does have a good idea," she said. "Maybe we could even make it a steak fry."

"Sounds fine," agreed Mr. Smith. "Who knows, it might even be a little cooler there. In fact, I think I'll go talk to the porter right now to see about renting some carriages. Shall we set tomorrow for this big event?"

"Oh, Daddy," exclaimed Jeannie, "wait till I tell Tim!" She turned and dashed out the door with Toby right at her heels.

The next day, the early morning sun streamed through Jeannie's window.

"Yip! Yip!" Toby sat by the door, his head cocked to one side.

Jeannie sat up, rubbing her eyes. "So you're all ready for the steak fry?" she laughed. "Guess that makes me a slowpoke. I'd better get up and help Mother."

Hanging her nightgown in the wardrobe, she pulled her dress over her head. She brushed her light brown hair back and tied a wide yellow ribbon around it. Yellow was a good color for a picnic, she thought. She grabbed her big straw hat, and she and Toby bounded down two flights of stairs to the dining room.

All morning people were rushing around the hotel. Jeannie's mother was down in the kitchen helping the hotel cooks pack the cakes and the breads and, of course, the steaks. They poured lemonade into large glass bottles. By noon everything was ready.

Three carriages and two wagons rolled up the driveway. The drivers hopped down and tied the horses to the hitching posts. All the ladies held parasols over their heads to shade themselves from the hot sun. The girls stood together in little groups. Tim and the other older boys stuck their hands in their pockets and watched the smaller boys race up and down the porch steps. The fathers were busy loading the baskets into the wagons and talking to the drivers.

Finally Father called out, "Let's get started." Climbing up into the back of a wagon and clutching Toby in her arms, Jeannie saw her brother, Tim.

"Come sit next to me, Tim," she called.

"Okay," agreed Tim as he climbed in beside her. "I see you really did bring that dumb dog."

"I keep telling you, Tim, he's not a dumb dog," said Jeannie. She held Toby on her lap so the little dog could see over the side of the wagon.

The five vehicles headed down the hill and rumbled across the wooden bridge over Monument Creek. The road led up the creek bank and onto the mesa. Jeannie didn't see much except yucca and a few cottonwood trees. The soil was very red. The hot sun beat down through her thin cotton dress. Toby sat in her lap, panting.

After a while the lead wagon started down a steep road leading off the top of the mesa. The others followed. As they came to the bottom, they stopped by a little stream. The drivers climbed down and started to unhitch the teams.

Jeannie jumped out. Toby was right behind her. "Oh, look over there, Toby," she said, pointing to a group of huge pink rocks just ahead. "I'll bet those rocks are in the Garden of the Gods. Don't some of them look just like giant mushrooms, Toby?" The little dog wagged his tail.

"Oh, I think this is going to be a wonderful place for a picnic, Toby," added Jeannie. But Toby was running ahead, sniffing every bush as he went. "Don't go too far," she warned. "You might get lost out here in this strange place." But Toby was out of sight.

Just then Tim called, "Jeannie, come help gather firewood. We have to get lots to cook the steaks."

Father and the other men were chopping up pieces of dried cottonwood lying by the stream. The boys and girls played hide-and-seek as they looked for brush and twigs.

Soon a big pile of logs and brush lay on the bare ground by the stream. "How long will it take to get the fire going, Alfred?" asked Mother.

"Oh, a little while, dear," he answered. "Long enough for the children to play some games. How about some races, Jeannie?"

"Oh, yes," agreed Jeannie. "Boys against girls."

"That's dumb!" said Tim. "Boys always beat the girls, and then the girls just get mad."

Is that so?" answered Jeannie. "I can beat you any old time."

"All right, you two," said Father. "I think choosing teams is the best idea. Jeannie, you and Tim can be captains. And remember—boys and girls on each team."

Soon all twelve boys and girls were chosen. Even little Nancy Bean who was only five.

"Now this will be a relay race," explained Father. "Each team will have a stick which every runner must hold and pass on to the next runner on his team. You must run up to those first big pink rocks and come back here."

Both teams lined up behind the starting line. The mothers and fathers stood nearby. Jeannie and Tim gripped their sticks.

Jeannie placed her foot right behind the starting line Father had drawn in the dirt. She was ready. But then she remembered Toby. Where could he be? Just as she started to look around, Father raised one hand above his head. "Are you ready?" he called out. "On your mark. Get set. Go!"

Jeannie and Tim dashed up the road toward the rocks. Just as they made the turn, Jeannie saw Toby racing toward her.

"Toby, get out of the way!" she called.

"You'll get stepped on."

The little dog stopped for a minute, panting and watching Jeannie run by. Then he turned and walked slowly back into the underbrush.

Jeannie raced to the finish line. The next member of her team was ready, reaching for the stick Jeannie held in her hand.

"Come on, Bob!" Jeannie called out, as she tried to catch her breath. She was too excited to notice the dark clouds moving across the sky and the wind blowing through the trees.

"Hurrah!" shouted Jeannie as the last member of her team ran across the finish line. "We won, we won!"

"We'll win the next race," answered her

brother. "Just you wait and see."

"I'm afraid we'll have to run that race another time," said Father. "The weather seems to be getting bad. We'll have to cook our steaks and start back right away."

Mother and other ladies were trying to keep the cloths from blowing off the long board set up as a table. The men were busy frying steaks. The smell of the meat sizzling over the glowing charcoal made Jeannie hungry.

But even as Jeannie went to get a plate, she could feel a few rain drops on her arms. Still she was going to eat every bit of her steak, she thought. She looked around for Toby. She wanted to give him her steak bone to chew, and she knew he was afraid of storms.

Very soon everyone hurried to help put dishes back into baskets and load everything into the carriages and wagons. Now the rain was pouring down.

The drivers hitched up the frightened horses. "Come on, everyone," called Father. "We'll have to make a dash back to the hotel."

But Jeannie was running around looking for Toby. "Toby! Toby!" she called.

"Jeannie, dear," shouted her father over the roar of the wind. "Get into the wagon, we have to go right now."

"But Daddy," said Jeannie, "Toby is lost. I have to find him."

"Toby will catch up to us, Jeannie," answered Father. "I don't like the looks of this storm. We have to leave right now. Toby is a smart dog. I'm sure he can even find his way back to the hotel. Now get in the wagon."

Jeannie climbed in, squeezing next to Tim. All around them were baskets and boxes from the picnic.

The drivers slapped the backs of the horses with the reins and off they went. The carriages and wagons lurched up the steep road. Jeannie peered back through the rain, but she couldn't see the little dog.

The wagon swayed along the bumpy road. Jeannie and Tim hung on to the baskets to keep them from bouncing out. Jeannie's dress was soaked and a stream of water ran down her nose.

Then Jeannie thought she heard a noise. "Tim, what was that?" she asked. "Don't you hear something funny?"

"Oh, you just hear the wind," answered Tim.

"No, no," said Jeannie. "Listen, there it is again. Like a dog whining."

"That's silly," said Tim. "The only dog is Toby and he's somewhere back where we had the picnic."

"I guess you're right," nodded Jeannie sadly. "Still, I sure thought I heard a dog."

The carriages and wagons rattled back across Monument Creek and raced up the hill toward the hotel. Jeannie and Tim had to hang on tight. As they turned into the driveway, the driver of their wagon pulled the frightened horses to a sudden stop. Boxes slid toward the back of the wagon and one large basket tumbled to the ground.

The top of the basket fell open and out peeked a small furry head.

"Yip! Yip!" came a sharp bark.

Jeannie leaped over the side of the wagon. "Toby, it's you! Oh, Toby!" She scooped him up and hugged him tight. The little dog wagged his tail and licked Jeannie's cheeks.

"Oh, Tim," exclaimed Jeannie, "isn't it wonderful? Toby is all right!" Still holding the small dog tight in her arms, she turned to walk up the steps with Tim.

Suddenly she heard a deep voice saying, "And where did that little fellow come from?" Father and Mother were laughing as they tried to wring some of the water out of their wet clothes.

"Toby hid in one of the baskets, Daddy," Jeannie explained.

As Tim held the big front door open, he started to laugh too. "One thing is for sure, Jeannie," he said, "you can't say we haven't had plenty of exciting things happen today."

"And, Tim, you can't say that Toby isn't a smart dog either," added Father.

"In fact, he's smarter than all of us, I guess," said Jeannie. "Just look at him. Dry as a bone. Why, he's the only one who had sense enough to keep out of the rain."

The Diamond Back

Greeley, Colorado
June 1887

Ingrid Andersen picked up her carpetbag and climbed down the steep steps of the railroad car.

"Stay right behind me, Ingrid," warned her older brother, Sven, speaking in Swedish. "I don't want you getting lost now that we're finally here."

Ingrid and Sven had made the long trip from their home in Sweden to work on the Fairchild farm just outside the little town of Greeley. Times were hard in Sweden, and the Andersens could not feed all their big family. So they decided that the two oldest children—Sven, seventeen, and Ingrid, thirteen—would go to America to work.

At first the platform of the railway station was full of people, bustling here and there. But soon Ingrid and Sven stood all alone.

"You don't think the Fairchilds have forgotten us, Sven?" asked Ingrid.

But before Sven could answer, a buckboard rattled up the dirt street. A large woman got down and tied the team to the hitching post. Quickly she dusted off her dress and tucked stray wisps of brown hair back into the rest pinned up on top of her head.

"Sven Andersen?" she asked as she saw the two standing there.

"Mrs. Fairchild?" answered Sven.

"Yes, I'm Mrs. fairchild," she answered. "Sorry I couldn't meet your train. Just so much to do out at the farm. Sure glad you're here. My, how we need your help, young man."

"Yes, ma'am," answered Sven. "And, Mrs. Fairchild, this is my sister, Ingrid."

Mrs. Fairchild turned to look at Ingrid for the first time. "Ingrid?" she asked. "I didn't send for a girl. Goodness knows, what with my three little girls and my being a widow, we already have too many girls."

Ingrid listened carefully to what Mrs. Fairchild and Sven were saying. She didn't know much English yet, and she couldn't understand some of the words.

Finally she tugged at Sven's sleeve. "Sven," she whispered, "what are you saying?"

But Sven shrugged off her hand and kept talking to Mrs. Fairchild.

"I know you did not send for a girl, Mrs. Fairchild," he said. "But Ingrid is a hard worker. She is a good cook, too."

Ingrid heard her name and she knew about cooking. "Ja," she said, smiling. "I cook good. You bet."

But Mrs. Fairchild frowned and shook her head. "No, Sven," she said. "I'm afraid Ingrid cannot stay. There are some Swedish families who live over in Ryssby, a town not far from the mountains. I will write to the minister of the church there. I'm sure he can find a good home for her." Sven hung his head.

"But for now," Mrs. Fairchild went on,

"Ingrid can come and stay with us. So come along."

She turned and led Ingrid and Sven over to the buckboard. "You both come sit up here with me," she said.

As Sven flung their two bags in the back of the wagon, Ingrid pulled on his sleeve again. "Can I stay, Sven?" she asked. "Is it all right?"

"No, it is not all right," he answered gruffly. "The lady says you cannot stay."

Ingrid stared at her brother. "Not stay?" she asked. "But where will I go? What will I do?"

"I will think of something," answered Sven. "Now we are going out to the farm. Do not worry. It will be all right." He gave her shoulder a pat.

Mrs. Fairchild untied the horses and climbed up onto the seat. When Ingrid and Sven were settled beside her, she flicked the reins and they started down the street.

"Lots of trees," said Sven, as they moved along. "That is good."

"Yes, indeed," answered Mrs. Fairchild. "And see how wide the streets are? One hundred feet, including the sidewalks. At least twice as wide as most streets."

"And water. Over there," added Sven.

"Sure," nodded Mrs. Fairchild. "Have to have water. Every street in town has a ditch like

Greeley—*Courtesy Colorado Historical Society*

that to bring water to the folks' gardens."

"Ja," said Sven, "that is a fine idea. Look, Ingrid." He pointed to the ditch as the buckboard rolled along. But Ingrid couldn't see anything. Her eyes were filled with tears.

"Fact is, Sven," Mrs. Fairchild went on, "all the land around here has to be watered. Just not enough rain, you see. So when my husband first came out here back in 1870 with the other colonists, he helped to dig the main irrigation ditch. It carries water from the streams called the Big and Little Thompson and the St. Vrain."

Sven nodded as Mrs. Fairchild kept telling all about the early days of Greeley or the Union Colony as she said it was once called. But Ingrid heard nothing. As they bumped along, she could only think of leaving Sven. How could she get along? What would she do?

Then suddenly Ingrid saw that they were out of town. The land was a little hilly and there were no trees. Not green and pretty like Sweden, she thought. But as long as she was with Sven everything was all right.

"Not much farther now," Mrs. Fairchild said. "You can see the house from here." She pointed ahead of her.

Ingrid cupped her hands around her eyes. Squinting in the bright sun, she could just see the small wooden house. To one side was a large shed. A barbed wire fence circled the buildings.

"Don't have any cattle," explained Mrs. Fairchild. "My husband was a farmer. This is fine land for growing things. Just have eighty acres. But that's almost too much for me to take care of myself."

"What do they grow, Sven?" asked Ingrid quietly.

Mrs. Fairchild looked over at the girl. "What's that she says?" asked Mrs. Fairchild. "I don't understand a word of Swedish."

"Ingrid asked what you grow," Sven explained.

"Oh, mostly potatoes, wheat, and alfalfa. Raise some chickens and turkeys too," said Mrs. Fairchild. "And by the side of the house is my vegetable garden. Peas, beans, tomatoes. Things to can and eat over the winter. But it's just a mess of weeds now. No time to take care of it, I'm afraid."

As they rolled into the yard, Ingrid could see the little garden. A dingy, whitewashed picket fence was built around it. Ingrid felt sad to see the prickly weeds and grass choking the young plants.

Suddenly from around the corner dashed three girls. They all ran up to Sven.

"My name is Rhonda," said one little girl with curly brown hair. "I'm seven. Caroline is ten. And the baby, Julie, is three. Almost four."

"I'm not a baby," said the little girl. Her pale blond hair was wound into two little pigtails.

"You're Sven, aren't you?" asked Rhonda.

"Ja," he answered, "and this is Ingrid, my sister."

"Oh, I didn't think a girl was coming too," said the oldest girl, Caroline. "That's nice. Now we have someone new to play with, Mother."

"Another playmate is not what we need here, girls," Mrs. Fairchild said sternly. "It's more help in the fields we need. So Ingrid will be moving on just as soon as I can find her a nice home."

"Oh, Mother," begged Rhonda, "can't she stay? P-lease!"

"No," said her mother. "Caroline, I hope you have the stew warmed up because we have to eat and get back out to fix some of the irrigation ditches."

"Yes, Mother," answered Caroline, "Everything is ready. Only we don't have any bread."

"Can't be helped. No time to bake," answered Mrs. Fairchild. As she started into the house, she turned toward Ingrid and Sven. "You know, I plum forgot my manners. Ingrid, you put your things in the house. You can sleep with the two older girls. Sven, we fixed you a nice room in the shed. While you all get settled, I'll serve up the dinner."

Sven turned to his sister and quietly told her what Mrs. Fairchild had just said. "No, no," said Ingrid. "I serve dinner. You rest, lady."

"What?" asked Mrs. Fairchild. "Oh, well, yes. All right. That would be nice. Thank you, Ingrid."

Ingrid saw a long apron hanging on a hook on the door. She took it down and tied it around her skirt. She dished the thick stew into crockery bowls and placed them on the table. Rhonda brought out a pitcher of milk from the cooler. Everyone sat down to eat.

"Sorry about the bread," said Mrs. Fairchild.

"I bake, lady," said Ingrid, smiling. "After dinner. No?"

Mrs. Fairchild wiped her mouth with her napkin. She looked at Ingrid carefully. "You sure you know how to make sourdough bread?" she asked.

"Ja," answered Ingrid.

"Well, all right," agreed Mrs. Fairchild. "I guess it won't hurt to let you try. But right now it's time for the rest of us to get out there to the ditches."

"Can I go, too, Mommy?" asked little Julie, her round face barely peeking up over the edge of the table.

"No, dear," said Mrs. Fairchild. "We have work to do. You stay here with Ingrid."

Ingrid had already cleared the table and started washing the dishes before everyone left. She saw the broom in the corner and quickly brushed the wooden floor clean. Mrs. Fairchild had shown her the sourdough starter to use to make the bread. Now Ingrid put the glob into a large mixing bowl. She added flour and water and carefully mixed it all together. Placing a clean cloth over the top, she put it on the kitchen table. After supper tonight, it would be ready to make into loaves and bake.

"Come, Julie," she said. "We go beat weeds in garden."

Julie giggled. "You talk funny, Ingrid," she said. "But I like you. I can get you the hoe."

The little girl ran over to the shed and soon returned, carrying the hoe. "Thank you," said Ingrid. "Now, hat for you, please."

"Hat?" said Julie. "Oh, I don't need a hat."

"Hat," said Ingrid again. "Hot today. You get hat."

"Oh, all right," said Julie as she slowly went back into the house.

Ingrid pushed open the gate and went into the vegetable garden. She hardly knew where to start. Weeds were everywhere. She thought the peas would be a good place to begin.

Julie came into the garden carrying a rag doll under her arm. She walked down to the other end of the garden and sat in the shade of

the lilac bush.

Ingrid could feel her dress sticking to her back as she worked in the hot afternoon sun. She was happy to see how nice the pea vines looked now without a weed around them. Soon she would have the little bean plants done.

Then out of the corner of her eye she saw something. Maybe a long branch lying in the warm dirt. But her heart stopped. She saw it was no branch, but a snake. She stood very still and watched it. About four feet long, the snake had diamond shaped blotches edged with yellow running along its back. Its tail looked like it was made from small parts glued together.

Ingrid didn't move, and neither did the snake. She hoped it was asleep. For a second she looked up and saw Julie, sitting at the other end of the garden. She was humming as she played with her doll. Ingrid was sure that if either she or Julie moved, the snake would wake up.

As Ingrid stood there, gripping her hoe, she had an idea. Carefully, slowly, she took a step closer to the snake. It still did not move. Good. Ingrid knew she was strong for her age. But would she be strong enough?

She raised the hoe above her head. With one quick stroke, she brought the edge of the hoe down, bashing the snake on the head. She beat the snake again and again. She could hear Julie crying. But she kept slamming the hoe down.

Then Ingrid realized the head of the snake was cut off from its body. Julie ran up and Ingrid put her arms around the little girl.

"You saved us, Ingrid," cried Julie. "You saved us from that bad old rattler. I think you're the bravest girl in the world."

Ingrid smiled and wiped the little girl's tears away with the corner of her apron. She saw that her own hands were shaking. Then she felt a hand on her shoulder.

Ingrid turned and saw Mrs. Fairchild. Caroline and Rhonda were trotting behind Sven.

"What happened?" Sven gasped, when he

saw the dead snake stretched out in the dirt.

"I killed it, Sven," explained Ingrid. "I knew it would hurt little Julie."

"But it could have killed you, little sister," said Sven. "That was a dangerous thing for you to do."

"Don't you know rattlesnakes are poisonous, Ingrid?" asked Mrs. Fairchild.

"Ja," nodded Ingrid.

"Well, young lady," said Mrs. Fairchild, "you are very brave, indeed. And very strong too, I see. There's not much left of that snake."

She stood with her hands on her hips and looked around the garden. "How nice everything looks in here too," said Mrs. Fairchild, smiling.

"Can Ingrid stay now, Mommy?" begged Julie.

"I would be so happy too," added Sven, hopefully.

"W-ell," began Mrs. Fairchild, "I don't know. I just hadn't planned on another girl. But, then, I guess Ingrid is not just another girl."

"Ingrid is the most special girl," exclaimed Caroline, giving Ingrid a hug.

"Yes, Caroline, I think you're right," agreed Mrs. Fairchild. "A most special girl indeed."

"I stay?" asked Ingrid again, hardly daring to breathe.

"Yes, you stay," Mrs. Fairchild nodded.

Ingrid looked around at the three girls and

Mrs. Fairchild. Sven stood there, grinning. "Thank you, lady," Ingrid said, very softly. "I be the hardest working girl in America. But most of all, I be the happiest girl in all America."

The Bottom of the Barrel

Steamboat Springs, Colorado
Fall 1907

Charlie Dunn placed the geranium plants in the front window of the little store.

"What do you think, Ma?" he asked.

"Why, I think they add a real nice touch, Charlie," said his mother. "Makes the window look right pretty."

"Maybe the flowers will make people stop at our store," said Charlie. "Here it is Saturday afternoon. Shopping day for all the ranchers and town folks too. But I'll bet we've only had half a dozen customers."

"I'll admit business is a bit slow, Charlie," said his mother. "But we just opened, remember. Folks don't know about us yet."

"I guess you're right, Ma," said Charlie. "But you would think folks would want to try a new store. Not always going to Withers' or Hugus' stores."

"Of course, that's what your father and I thought when we opened the store," admitted Mrs. Dunn.

Charlie and his mother and father had moved from Leadville to Steamboat Springs, thinking the growing town would be a good place for a store. Charlie liked the way the town was right on the Yampa River. Lots of good fishing there. Dad told him how this valley was Ute Indian country up until about twenty-five years ago when the Utes were moved to reservations. Seems like the Utes and even the old fur trappers liked the hot sulphur springs that bubbled up even now all over town.

But today Steamboat Springs was a busy place. Two newspapers, three banks, electric lights. The Moffat Railroad came all the way from Denver—175 miles.

"You know, Ma," said Charlie, "maybe we should sell something different from the other stores. Something besides stuff like coffee, boots, and plows." He stared out the big window and watched the buggies and wagons drive along Lincoln Street right past the store.

Just then Charlie heard the chugging of an automobile outside. It stopped in front of the store. Must be the Chambers, he thought. The Chambers had the biggest ranch in the Yampa Valley, and they were the only ones rich enough to buy an automobile. Besides, Mrs. Chambers liked new things like automobiles.

Mrs. Chambers stepped out of the automobile and opened the door to the store. Charlie

Steamboat Springs 1908—Courtesy Colorado Historical Society

couldn't help noticing how she was dressed. His mother and the other ladies always talked about the clothes Mrs. Chambers wore. Talk was that her clothes came all the way from Chicago.

"Afternoon, Mrs. Chambers," said Mrs. Dunn.

"Good afternoon," answered Mrs. Chambers. "Lovely Fall day, isn't it?"

"Indeed it is," answered Charlie's mother. "And what can we do for you?"

"Well, quite frankly," said Mrs. Chambers, "this is the first time I've been in your store. I love new things, you know, and I've been meaning to come in long before this." The tall woman looked around her carefully.

"What is in the barrel?" asked Mrs. Chambers, pointing to the large barrel sitting on the floor at the end of the counter.

"Pickles, Mrs. Chambers," answered Charlie. "My father has a special way of making them."

Mrs. Chambers turned to look at Charlie. "Does he really?" she asked. "You don't suppose I could have a sample?"

"You sure can," said Charlie. He took the wooden ladle off the hook on the barrel. He lowered it into the huge barrel filled with brine and pickles. In a moment, he brought up a large pickle. He let the liquid drip off. Then he carefully handed it to Mrs. Chambers.

As she held the big pickle between her fingers, she took a small bite. Then a much bigger bite. "M-m-m," she said. "Really delicious!" She wiped her fingers carefully with her lace handkerchief.

"You are right, young man," said Mrs. Chambers. "That is a very special pickle. Everyone in town should know about these pickles. In fact, I think I should buy some for my little boy. Robert dearly loves pickles."

As Charlie wrapped the pickles in brown paper, Mrs. Chambers looked in the long mirror. She took one of the large hat pins out of her hat. Then tilting the hat just a little, she put the pin back in the hat.

"Such a lovely hat, if I may say so, Mrs. Chambers," said Charlie's mother. "I do so admire your hats."

"Why, thank you," said Mrs. Chambers, smiling. "I find the hats for sale here in Steamboat Springs are just not to my liking. So I must get them when Mr. Chambers and I go to Denver or Chicago."

Charlie handed Mrs. Chambers her package. The tall woman gave a little wave and went out the door. Charlie watched Mr. Chambers crank the car engine and in a few minutes they were chugging down the street.

As Charlie was sweeping out the store that night, he thought of Mrs. Chambers. Mostly he thought of Mrs. Chambers' hat. It certainly was different from the hats the other ladies wore. Even he could see that. Mrs. Chambers' hat was much bigger and there wasn't a flower on it. That must be the fashion.

All day Sunday and even at school on Monday, Charlie thought about that big hat. That afternoon as he walked in the back door of the store, he called out, "Ma, I know just what we should do."

"Do about what, Charlie?" asked his mother.

"We should sell ladies' hats," said Charlie.

"You know, like Mrs. Chambers wears. Then I'd bet folks would come into the store."

"Charlie, if you don't beat all!" exclaimed his mother. "A son of mine thinking about ladies' hats. But you know, I think you have a good idea. In fact, your father is just about to make a trip into Denver to buy some things for the store. I'll just cut out some pictures from Vogue magazine and he can buy a few. Then we can see how they sell." She gave Charlie a hug.

Charlie felt good as he worked around the store that afternoon. Maybe his idea would help. Suddenly the door burst open and five little boys ran in. One of them was Robert Chambers. Charlie knew him from school.

"We've come for pickles, Charlie," said the boy with bright red hair and a face full of freckles. "I know you've got 'em. Mother brought some home a couple of days ago."

"Sure your Mother knows you're buying pickles?" asked Charlie, leaning over the counter.

"Oh, she doesn't mind," said Robert. "I can have anything I want."

"Well," began Charlie. "I don't know."

"Oh, I'm sure it would be all right," chuckled Mrs. Dunn.

"Okay," said Charlie. He reached for the wooden ladle and began to spoon out pickles.

"Wait," said Robert. "I want to get my own."

"But the pickles are way at the bottom, Robert," explained Charlie. "You're too little to reach that far down."

"Oh, I can do it," he said. "You just wait and see."

Robert pulled himself up onto the counter and stretched out full length. His arms, head and shoulders were hanging over the edge—over the huge barrel.

"I'm all set," said Robert. "Now hand me the ladle, and I'll just reach in and fish out a pickle. Simple."

Robert squirmed a little farther over the edge. His head and shoulders were into the barrel. Using both hands, he plunged the ladle deep down into the barrel. Suddenly Robert's feet kicked wildly. And then—splash! Robert fell headfirst into the huge barrel!

Robert's friends jumped up and down, laughing. Charlie reached in and pulled the boy out of the barrel. His hair was dripping with pickle brine. His shirt was streaked with brown stains from the barrel.

"You all right, Robert?" asked Charlie, anxiously.

"Sure," answered Robert. "And look, I told you I'd get the biggest pickle." Proudly, he held up his prize.

Just then Mrs. Chambers strode into the store. She stopped short as she saw Robert. She looked over at Charlie. Charlie held his breath.

"What in the world happened?" she asked.

"I got the biggest pickle, Mother," answered Robert, taking another bite.

"Oh, Robert, just look at you!" she moaned.

The other boys were quiet now. Except for the crunch of Robert chewing his pickle, there was not a sound in the room.

Then Mrs. Chambers put her hands on her hips and began to laugh. "Oh, Robert! If you aren't the funniest sight I've ever seen! Can you imagine a son who likes pickles so much he will fall into a barrel to get one!"

She turned to Charlie. "You know, young man," she said. "I think you really have something here in your new store. The best pickles in town! I wouldn't be surprised if you saw quite a lot of Robert and his friends from now on."

"That would be swell, Mrs. Chambers," said Charlie. "Of course, we sure would like you to come in, too."

"Oh, you can count on it," said Mrs. Chambers, as she led Robert out the door.

Charlie didn't even mind cleaning up the mess around the pickle barrel. Now that Mrs. Chambers was coming to the store, other folks would come, too. And maybe, just maybe, Mrs. Chambers would buy one of their new hats.

Glossary

Mountain City: an early name for Central City, Colorado

Terrier: a small dog, first used to chase game and to root the animals out of their holes

Carpetbag: a bag used for traveling, usually made of heavy rug-like material

Ja: "Yes," in Swedish

Starter: a small piece of dough saved from one batch to "start" or help the next batch of dough to rise.

Brine: a salt and water solution for pickling

Bibliography

Treasure from the Ashes

Hill, David G. "The Negro in the Early West," *The Iliff Review*, Vol. 3. No. 3, 1946.

The Historical Encyclopedia of Colorado, Denver: Colorado Historical Association, 1975.

History of the City of Denver, Arapahoe County and Colorado, Chicago: O. L. Baskin & Co., 1880.

King, Neil L. *History of Banking in Denver, Colorado, 1858-1950*. Thesis for the Graduate School of Banking, American Bankers Association of Rutgers University, New Brunswick, Rhode Island, 1952.

Mothershead, Harmon. "Negro Rights in Colorado Territory," *Colorado Magazine*, Vol. 40, July 1963.

Parkhill, Forbes. *Mister Barney Ford*, Denver: Sage Books, 1963.

Wharton, J. E. *History of the City of Denver*, Denver: Eastwood Kirchner Printing Co., 1909.

Map of the Denver City, 1860, North of Cherry Creek, constructed by Edgar C. McMechin, State Historical Society.

Dry as a Bone

Buckman, George Rex. *Colorado Springs, Colorado and its Famous Scenic Environs*, Denver: W. H. Jackson Photo and Publishing Co., 1893

Ellis, Amanda M. *The Colorado Springs Story*, Colorado Springs: The House of San Juan, 1954.

Hall, Francesca Tudor. *Colorado Springs 52 Years Ago: An Analysis of the Population of El Paso County and Colorado Springs in 1885 and a Description and History of the City of Colorado Springs in the Same Year.* A Thesis for the Department of History, Colorado College, Colorado Springs, Colorado.

Robert, Edward. *Colorado Springs and Manitou*, Denver, Republic Printing Co., 1883.

Stone, Wilbur Fiske. ed. *History of Colorado*, Vol. I, Chicago: S. J. Clarke Publishing Company, 1918.

The Diamond Back

Boyd, David. *History of Greeley and the Union Colony of Colorado*, Greeley: the Greeley Tribune Press, 1890

Clark, J. Max. *Colonial Days*, Denver: The Smith-Brooks Co., 1902.

Farming in Colorado, Greeley: The Greeley Board of Trade, Sun Publishing Co., 1887.

Smith, Barbara. *1870-1970, the First 100 Years: Greeley, Colorado*, Greeley: the Journal Publishing Co., 1970.

Willard, James F. ed. *The Union Colony at Greeley, Colorado 1868-1871*, Denver, W. F. Robinson Printing Co., 1918

The Bottom of the Barrel

Burroughs, John Rolfe. *Steamboat in the Rockies*, Fort Collins, Colorado: Old Army Press, 1974.

Leckenby, Charles H. *The Tread of Pioneers*, Steamboat Springs, Colorado: Pilot Press, 1944.

Metcalf, F. A. *Steamboat Springs and Routt County*, 1906.

Notes

Treasure from the Ashes

The present site of Denver was laid out in October, 1858, and briefly called St. Charles. Only one month later, however, the name was changed to Denver after the Governor of Kansas, General J. W. Denver. Originally the west side of Cherry Creek, Auraria, attracted the majority of people and business. But by the time the Territorial Legislature granted the town of Denver a charter, the center of growth had changed to the east side of the Creek. Because almost all the buildings and homes were wooden, the disastrous fire of 1863 was not unexpected. All rebuilding that followed was done in brick. Barney Ford, who was born a slave in Virginia in 1820 and who escaped to Chicago via the underground railroad in 1848, was a valuable addition to the booming trading center of Denver. Despite the Black Laws of the Carolinas which had prohibited any slave learning to read or write, Ford had taught himself to read and do mathematics. By the time he arrived in Colorado in 1860, he was not only extremely well read and able to quote passages from

Shakespeare at length, but he was respected for his thoughtful and honest approach to the problems of the day. He became a leader of the Black people in Colorado and influential in gaining the right to vote. He became the owner of a number of successful restaurants and hotels in Colorado and Wyoming. He died in 1902. Luther Kountz joined his brother to found the Colorado National Bank.

Dry as a Bone

When General William J. Palmer organized the Denver & Rio Grande Company to extend the railroad south from Denver, it was his intention that it run through the ten thousand acre piece of land which he had purchased just east of Pikes Peak. The town would be known as Colorado Springs. General Palmer's Fountain Colony would sell membership to any person who was of good character, had strict temperance habits, and could pay $100. The first stake was driven on July 31, 1871 at Pikes Peak and Cascade Avenue. The principal reasons for Colorado Springs' early existence were its beautiful scenery and excellent climate. Visitors came from all over the world, and up until the mining boom of the 1890s two-thirds of the permanent population was there for health reasons. By 1885, the seven thousand cottonwood trees planted by the early colonists were shading the broad streets that ran two miles north and south and one mile east and west. The Antlers Hotel, built at a cost of $150,000, opened in 1881. The five-story hotel boasted seventy-five "large, airy rooms," electric bells, fire escapes, hot and cold water, and even Turkish baths. Although the hotel burned in 1898, it has been rebuilt twice.

The Diamond Back

The Union Colony, or Greeley, was organized in New York City by Nathan C. Meeker, the agricultural editor of the *New York Tribune* and Horace Greeley, owner of the newspaper. In the summer of 1869, Greeley visited Colorado and was very impressed with the natural resources and farming possibilities. The site of twelve thousand acres, located at the confluence of the South Platte and the Cache la Poudre rivers, was purchased from the Denver Pacific Railroad and some individuals. Fifty families drew up the town plan in which they divided it into business lots, residence lots, land for schools, churches, and public buildings. Adjacent land was divided into plats from five to one hundred twenty-five acres, according to the distance from town. Each member was entitled to a parcel of land for farming and the right to buy a lot in town. On one side of each street within the town ran an irrigation ditch to carry water for the trees and for family gardens. Greeley had over one hundred miles of irrigating canals and was often called "Garden City." By 1885, Greeley was an established community with a fire department, a nearly-completed electric light plant, a large library, schools, and many thriving businesses.

The Bottom of the Barrel

Early residents of Steamboat Springs talked of over one hundred thirty-eight mineral springs existing within the town's limits. The Yampa Valley, in which Steamboat Springs is located, contains one of the most diverse groups of mineral springs known. Because of the healing qualities, the springs were often used by Indians and fur trappers. In the 1830s it is said that the mountain men watched one of the springs shoot a geyser of water some twenty feet into the air. It also made the chugging sound of a river steamboat, and they dubbed the area "steamboat springs." The beautiful valley had been Ute Indian land until they were removed to a reservation in 1879. Once vacant, the area attracted farmers and ranchers almost immediately. From

1883 the town grew until it was incorporated in 1900 and became the county seat of Routt County in 1912. In 1907 Steamboat Springs was already the central town of northwestern Colorado, serving the rich farms and ranches within hundreds of miles.